Pride and Prejudice

Based on the Novel by Jane Austen
Adapted by Laura Pritchett

SCHOLASTIC INC.
New York Toronto London Auckland Sydney
Mexico City New Delhi Hong Kong Buenos Aires

Illustrations
Fulvia Zambon

Developed by ONO Books in cooperation with Scholastic Inc.

Printed in the U.S.A.

ISBN 0-439-59808-7

1 2 3 4 5 6 7 8 9 10 23 12 11 10 09 08 07 06 05 04 03

Contents

Welcome to This Book

If you had to choose, would you marry for love or money? Most people today wouldn't think twice before answering "Love!"

Elizabeth Bennet feels the same way. But in her world, marriage has more to do with cold hard cash than flowers and romance. When some rich single men come to town, Elizabeth's mother couldn't be happier. Elizabeth and her sisters are all beauties. If only these men will look their way!

Will love rule the day or will money talk? Read on to find out.

Target Words For Elizabeth and Jane, dating was serious business. These words will help you understand why.

- **class:** a group of people who have about the same amount of money and education
  In the old days, people dated only those who belonged to their social class.
- **eligible:** being a proper and worthy choice
  The eligible men were rich, handsome, and single.
- **prejudice:** judging before getting all the facts
  People can have a prejudice about things such as appearance, wealth, or education.

Reader Tips Here's how to get the most out of this book.

- **Meet the Characters** Check out the characters on pages 6–7. Connect their names with their pictures as you read.
- **Compare/Contrast** When you compare, you tell how things are alike. When you contrast, you tell how things are different. Comparing and contrasting how the characters act will help you remember and organize the story's elements and details.

Meet the Characters

This love story takes place in England nearly two hundred years ago. Back then, the dating game had very different rules.

The Girls

Elizabeth Bennet
The smart one. She's spunky and pretty, too. Darcy has seemed to notice. Or does she just imagine it?

Jane Bennet
The quiet one. She's even prettier than Elizabeth. And Bingley has definitely noticed.

Lydia Bennet
The flirt. She's young and easily fooled by a fast-talking guy.

The Guys

Fitzwilliam Darcy

A rich, handsome, single man. Make that very rich. He is also a snob. But is there more to him than meets the eye?

Charles Bingley

Another rich, handsome, single man. And he's nice, too. His sister is a bit of a snob, like Darcy.

George Wickham

A handsome soldier. He seems charming. But he and Darcy share a secret. Which one of them is lying?

CHAPTER

1

New Men in Town

Mrs. Bennet has high hopes for her daughters.

"Have you heard, my dear, that the nearby **manor** has been rented?" Mrs. Bennet said one day, smiling slyly at her husband. "A young man has taken it. I mean a *wealthy* young man."

"What's his name?" asked Mr. Bennet, hardly looking up from behind his book.

"Mr. Bingley. And apparently he is single—what a fine thing for our girls!"

"How so?"

"Dear husband, how can you be so silly!? He must marry one of them. You go and pay him a visit right away, so he can be introduced to our family."

Mr. Bennet laughed. "I will do no such thing."

"But think of your daughters and their futures. Someone must provide for them."

"Perhaps I should just send him a letter advertising all five of them! I'll throw in a good word for Elizabeth."

"She is no better than the others. Jane is prettier. And what about Mary, Kitty, and Lydia?"

"They are all silly girls, but Elizabeth is the smartest by far."

"How can you speak this way about your own daughters? Oh, my poor nerves! You don't care about my nerves at all."

Mr. Bennet let out a deep sigh. "My dear, I am well acquainted with your nerves. I have been living with them for thirty years."

Mr. Bennet loved to tease his wife. It was one of his favorite hobbies. Luckily for him, Mrs. Bennet rarely got the joke. She was too busy with her own hobby, trying to get her five daughters married. It took all the cleverness she had.

Heads Up!

Find two words to describe Mrs. Bennet and two to describe Mr. Bennet. In what ways are they different?

Soon, Mrs. Bennet encountered a wonderful opportunity. A ball was being held in the nearby town of Meryton, and the **eligible** Mr. Bingley was going to be there.

Mrs. Bennet arrived at the ball, eager to show off her daughters. The younger girls, Mary, Kitty, and Lydia, loved the attention. They twirled their dresses and batted their eyes at all the young men.

Jane, the oldest daughter, did not show off at all. She danced and talked quietly, not realizing just how beautiful she looked. Mr. Bingley, however, realized it perfectly well. He made sure he danced with Jane whenever he could.

Elizabeth, who didn't like the idea of being put on display, sat off to the side with her friend, Charlotte. They watched the other guests from a distance and commented.

"Mr. Bingley seems quite charming and friendly," remarked Charlotte.

"His sister looks quite the opposite," said Elizabeth, eyeing the cold-looking woman who strode around the party with her chin in the air. "I'm afraid Miss Bingley does not seem very glad to see her brother enjoying Jane's company."

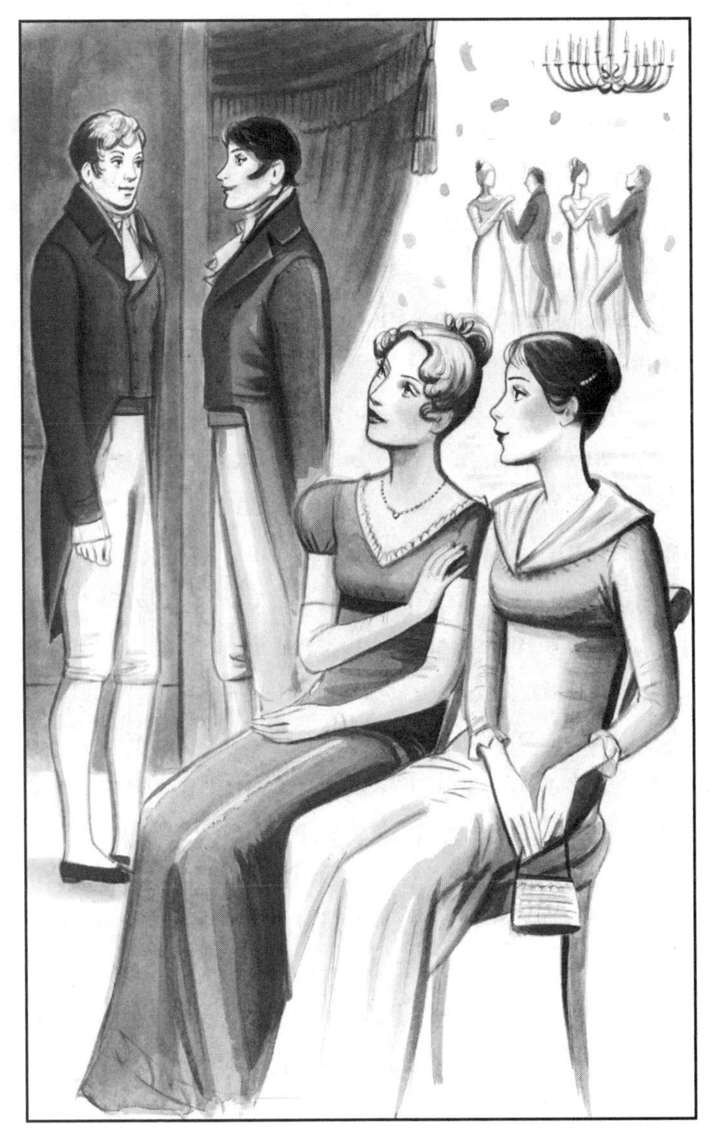

Elizabeth and Charlotte watch the other guests and comment.

Then Elizabeth caught the eye of a tall, dark-haired man who was even better looking than Mr. Bingley. The dark-haired man stood in a corner, tall and straight, looking rather stiff and uncomfortable.

Elizabeth looked away and asked Charlotte, "Who is the very handsome man over there who does not look at all like he is enjoying himself?"

"That is Mr. Darcy," said Charlotte. She leaned close and whispered, "I hear that he is visiting with Mr. Bingley. And he is even wealthier than his friend, I understand."

Just then, Bingley walked up to Darcy, and Elizabeth could just barely hear their conversation over the noise of the party.

"Darcy, you should dance!" said Bingley.

"I will not," said Darcy. "You know I don't like all this foolishness. Besides, there is not a woman here that I'd like to dance with."

"What about Elizabeth Bennet? Have you met her yet?"

"I have seen her," Darcy said, sounding bored, "And she is not pretty enough to tempt me."

Elizabeth blushed and turned away toward Charlotte. "Did you hear that?" she whispered. "How rude!"

Charlotte touched her friend on the shoulder. "I'm sure he didn't realize you could hear," she said. "But Elizabeth, you must remember that he does come from one of the wealthiest and most important families in England. He's not like us. He has a right to think that he's better."

"I could forgive his **pride** if he had not hurt mine," said Elizabeth, frowning.

When the ball was over, Elizabeth was more than happy to leave. She frowned as she listened to her mother talk nonstop about Bingley and Darcy all the way home. Meanwhile, Jane kept quiet and was smiling to herself. Elizabeth looked at Jane and thought it was wonderful that her favorite sister might be falling in love.

Heads Up!

Look up the word* pride *in the glossary at the end of the book. Is it a good quality or not? Why? Can you have too much pride?

CHAPTER

Mrs. Bennet's Plan

A rainstorm traps Jane at the Bingley mansion. How very convenient!

"It's for you," Elizabeth said with a sly smile, handing a letter to Jane, "and it happens to be from the Bingleys."

Jane tore the envelope open. "Oh, Elizabeth! Miss Bingley has invited me to come and spend the day at their manor."

"How wonderful to have a such a wealthy new friend," said Mrs. Bennet, beaming.

"May I go please, Mother?" Jane asked. "And may I please take the carriage?"

Mrs. Bennet thought for a moment, and then smiled slyly. "You may go, but I'd like you to ride the horse. It looks like it might rain, which means you will get wet. And then, of course, you will have to spend the night."

"*Mother!*" said Elizabeth, disgusted with her mother's plotting. "She'll catch a cold!"

"Good," said Mrs. Bennet. "Then she will have to stay several days, and Mr. Bingley can get to know her better."

In fact, just as Mrs. Bennet hoped, Jane arrived at the Bingley's wet and cold, and soon she developed a fever. The Bingleys sent her to bed and then notified Mrs. Bennet, who was very pleased with herself.

Elizabeth, however, was not at all pleased. The next day, she **trudged** three miles through the rain to the Bingley manor. She arrived at the door soaking wet, her dress splashed with mud. She greeted Mr. Bingley, Miss Bingley, and Mr. Darcy and then marched upstairs to check on her sister.

As soon as she had gone, Miss Bingley raised her chin in the air and said, "Can you imagine showing up at someone's home uninvited, looking such a mess? How very unlady-like."

"I thought Elizabeth looked just fine," said Mr. Bingley. "I think she must be very kind to go to all that trouble to be with her sister."

Elizabeth arrives soaking wet and splashed with mud.

"Yes," said Darcy. "Her eyes were bright from the walk."

"Her eyes!" said Miss Bingley, with a jealous laugh. "Are you admiring her, Mr. Darcy? When can I congratulate you?"

Darcy smiled. "Women are all alike," he said. "A man admires a woman, and they assume it's love; from there, they jump right to marriage in an instant."

"Well, anyway, I like *Jane* Bennet," said Miss Bingley. "But her family has no money—or manners, judging from the sister and the mother. Jane will never marry a **gentleman**."

The men said nothing, and turned away.

Elizabeth came back down when Jane fell asleep. Miss Bingley played the piano, while the others played cards and talked.

Heads Up!

What is Miss Bingley's impression of the Bennets? What kinds of things are important to Miss Bingley?

Elizabeth often looked up to find Darcy staring at her with his dark, intense eyes. She wondered if perhaps her hair did not look right. She already knew he didn't find her attractive, so why would he be staring at her like that?

Imagine her surprise, then, when Darcy asked her to dance. "Oh," she said, thinking fast, "You want me to say yes, but if I do, you will make fun of me for dancing. So I do not want to dance. Go ahead and **despise** me if you like."

"I do not despise you," said Darcy, sounding rather shocked to be refused in such a way. And yet, Elizabeth noticed that he did not lose interest in her. In fact, as the evening went on, he relaxed and often smiled at Elizabeth's jokes.

When the two sisters left the next day, Bingley and Darcy watched their carriage drive off. Bingley looked quite sad to see them go, but Darcy just stared. And as the sisters rode home, Elizabeth found she could not get this strange, handsome man out of her mind.

CHAPTER

A "Generous" Offer

Mr. Collins arrives and takes an interest in Elizabeth. Isn't she lucky?

The Bennets sat around the breakfast table one morning, shortly after the sisters had returned from the Bingleys'.

Mr. Bennet said to his wife, "I hope, my dear, that you will have a good dinner tonight, because someone will be joining us."

"Wonderful! Is our guest a single man?"

"No, no." Mr. Bennet said, shaking his head. "I have received a letter from Mr. Collins, who, as you may remember, is my cousin."

"Oh, do not mention his name in this house!"

"Yes, yes, he's the very man who will **inherit** this house someday. When I am dead, he can make you all leave as soon as he pleases."

"What an awful man! How can I face him?"

"Mama, it is not Mr. Collins's fault," said Elizabeth. "The law says that the house must pass to a man. It's simply too bad that all your children were foolish enough to be girls."

"In any case, Mr. Collins will be here at four o'clock," said Mr. Bennet.

Mr. Collins was a tall, heavy, young man, and indeed, he appeared at the door exactly on time. As soon as he came in the door, he began talking. He complimented the family's house. He complimented Mrs. Bennet on having such fine daughters. He complimented the chairs and rugs and everything else in every part of the house.

During dinner, he complimented the food and the room and the dining table. In fact, he never stopped talking. As soon as they were able, Mr. Bennet and his daughters excused themselves from his company.

Heads Up!

Until recent times, women weren't allowed to own property. That's one reason why Mrs. Bennet wants her daughters married to men who can take care of them.

When Mr. Collins was left entirely alone with Mrs. Bennet he turned to her and said knowingly, "I understand that my claim on this estate is a hardship to your daughters."

"They will be **destitute** if they do not marry," said Mrs. Bennet, trying her best to hide her dislike for the man.

"Well," replied Mr. Collins, "I intend to marry, and I am in a position to make a generous offer. I will marry one of your daughters. I have come to admire them quite a lot."

Mrs. Bennet brightened suddenly and began to beam at Mr. Collins.

He smiled back and said, "It is Jane's lovely face that strikes me most."

"Oh, but I must hint to you that Jane might soon be engaged," said Mrs. Bennet. "You see, there is a young man—"

"Fine, then." Mr. Collins cut her off. "Elizabeth is equal to Jane in beauty."

Mrs. Bennet smiled from ear to ear. I was wrong to think otherwise, now that I see what a fine man this Mr. Collins is, she thought to herself.

CHAPTER

Wickham's Woes

Why is this charming young man holding a grudge against Darcy?

The day after Mr. Collins's visit, the Bennet sisters decided to walk to Meryton. Lydia, the youngest sister, loved to flirt with the soldiers who were stationed there.

As soon as the sisters arrived, Lydia pulled them over to meet a soldier who was new to the troop. His name was Mr. Wickham. Elizabeth could not help thinking he was very good looking.

While Lydia flirted shamelessly, Elizabeth and Jane looked up to find Darcy and Bingley on horseback, coming down the street. It looked like the two men were about to stop and talk to them, but then Darcy caught sight of Mr. Wickham.

Darcy's face turned angry and Wickham's grew pale. They turned away from each other. Darcy

Darcy's face grows angry and Wickham's grows pale.

tipped his hat to the women, then rode on. Bingley waited there for a moment. He looked at Jane as though he wanted to stop, then he turned and rode to catch up with Darcy.

Elizabeth gazed after them, wondering what had just happened.

"You look surprised," Wickham said to her. "I have known Darcy's family since I was a baby. Unfortunately, we are not on good terms."

"But why?" Elizabeth asked.

"His father was one of the finest men that ever lived. He was my godfather and he promised me an inheritance. But when he died, Mr. Darcy kept the money for himself."

"Good heavens!" cried Elizabeth. "I never thought Mr. Darcy was as mean as that. He is a proud man, and I would think he would be ashamed to act so unfairly."

"He is, in fact, full of pride," replied Wickham. "But it does not serve him well."

"Is he ever kind?" Elizabeth asked.

"Yes, he often gives money to the poor. He is also very kind to his sister."

"What kind of girl is his sister?"

"Georgiana is a pretty girl, about sixteen."

Elizabeth wondered aloud, "I cannot believe that Mr. Bingley would be friends with such a dishonest man. He must not know all there is to know about Mr. Darcy."

"Probably not," said Mr. Wickham. "Mr. Darcy can be very pleasant when he wants to be."

The two kept talking, and Elizabeth found herself quite taken with Mr. Wickham. On the way home, she thought how kind he seemed and wondered how she could have ever thought that Mr. Darcy was charming.

Heads Up!

What do you think of Wickham's story? How does it make you feel about Darcy? How does it make Elizabeth feel?

CHAPTER

Bingley's Ball

Elizabeth has questions for Darcy and an answer for Mr. Collins.

Mr. Bingley's manor looked splendid to Elizabeth when she arrived several days later. Bingley was holding a ball, and the town had been looking forward to it for weeks.

Elizabeth was especially excited to dance with Mr. Wickham, but he was nowhere to be seen. Mr. Collins, however, was everywhere. He followed Elizabeth around like a puppy and insisted she dance with him. Elizabeth tried to smile while he dragged her around the dance floor and talked nonstop about his important friends.

When Elizabeth finally escaped his clutches, Mr. Darcy appeared and abruptly asked her to dance. She wondered why he was showing an interest in her, but she agreed out of politeness.

They danced in silence for quite a while. Finally, she said, "When you saw us the other day, we were just making a new friend."

The effect was immediate. Mr. Darcy blushed and said, "Mr. Wickham is good at making friends, but not at keeping them."

"I see that he has lost your friendship," said Elizabeth, hoping to get more information. Darcy made no answer. She went on, "Do you ever allow yourself to be blinded by **prejudice**, Mr. Darcy?"

"I hope not," said Darcy. "Why do you ask?"

"I hear people say many different things about you. I am only trying to understand."

Darcy did not reply, and when the dance was over, they left each other in awkward silence. At that moment, Miss Bingley came up to Elizabeth.

"I hear from your sisters that you have met Mr. Wickham," she said coldly. "I must warn you,

Heads Up!

look up* prejudice *in the glossary. What kind of prejudice do you think Elizabeth is talking about?

as a friend, not to trust him. Darcy has always been kind to him, but Wickham has treated Darcy in a terrible manner."

Elizabeth listened without believing a word Miss Bingley said. Before she could reply, she was distracted by a familiar voice across the room.

"Well, yes," her mother was announcing loudly to anyone who would listen, "Jane and Mr. Bingley are quite fond of each other. I suspect there will be an announcement soon..."

Miss Bingley turned to stare at Mrs. Bennet with disgust. Elizabeth looked around the room and noticed that many other people—including Darcy—were doing the same. She ducked her head in shame.

The next day proved to be just as bad for Elizabeth. Mr. Collins arrived unexpectedly at the Bennets' house and asked to have a moment alone to speak with her.

When they were alone, Mr. Collins cleared his throat, stuck out his chest, and said: "You can guess why I wish to see you. I have decided you shall be the one to marry me."

Elizabeth covered her mouth to hide a smile. She said, "I am honored by your proposal, but I must decline."

Mr. Collins laughed. "Oh, I understand that you ladies feel you must reject the first offer. I understand it's all part of the game."

"Mr. Collins," said Elizabeth, no longer smiling. "I am not a lady who plays games! You could not make me happy, and I could not make you happy either. So, I feel that there is no other answer I could offer you at later date."

Mr. Collins stared at Elizabeth in disbelief. He turned without saying a word and stormed out.

Mrs. Bennet was waiting for Elizabeth when she came out. "How do you expect to support yourself if you insist on refusing perfectly good offers? I will never speak to you again if you do not marry Mr. Collins."

"And I will never speak to you again if you do," said Mr. Bennet, winking at Elizabeth.

CHAPTER

Not Even a Good-bye

Jane is in love, but she is jilted. Charlotte gets married, but isn't in love.

Jane did her best to stop her tears as she slumped over a letter that had just arrived.

"Oh, Elizabeth," she said. "It's a letter from Miss Bingley. They have all left for London. And Mr. Bingley didn't even say good-bye."

Elizabeth took her sister's hand. "Jane, I can't believe it. I thought Mr. Bingley loved you."

"But then why did he leave?" Jane asked, her eyes brimming over with tears.

"If I were to guess, I would say his sister is responsible. I suspect she didn't want him to marry you. After all, our family is not rich enough or grand enough for her."

Jane bowed her head and began to cry. Elizabeth put her arms around her sister.

Jane learns that Bingley has gone to London without even saying good-bye.

"Oh, Jane," said Elizabeth, "I had always liked Mr. Bingley, but I have to think less of him now."

"I'm sure his sister thought only of his happiness," Jane said through her tears.

"That I do not believe. She thought only about wealth and importance, more likely." Elizabeth bowed her head. "The more I see of the world, the more I dislike it, and the more I think that most of the people in it are fools."

Later that day, a carriage pulled up and out climbed Charlotte. Elizabeth went outside to greet her friend, who had some shocking news.

"I've come to tell you, dear Elizabeth, that Mr. Collins has asked me to marry him."

Elizabeth stared in disbelief. "And you said yes? My dear Charlotte, it's impossible!"

"Why impossible?" Charlotte asked, sounding a little offended. "You don't think he could find another woman attractive?"

"No, no, it's not that," Elizabeth said.

"I can see what you are thinking, Elizabeth," said Charlotte. "He just proposed to you, after all, and I suppose I should feel like his second choice.

But I am not romantic, you know. I never was. All I want is a comfortable home, and I believe my chance of happiness with Mr. Collins is fair. I am older than you, after all. I am twenty-seven! If I do not marry soon, Elizabeth, I may not get married at all."

As she watched Charlotte go, Elizabeth could not help but feel sorry for her friend. What a bad match, she thought. She had always felt that Charlotte would want something better for herself. How awful for her to spend the rest of her life with someone she didn't love.

Heads Up!

Charlotte and Elizabeth look at marriage in different ways. Explain the difference in your own words.

CHAPTER

Escape to the City

The sisters go to London, and Darcy reappears.

The following months passed quickly. Jane left for London to stay with her favorite aunt and uncle, Mr. and Mrs. Gardiner. Elizabeth, meanwhile, saw a lot of Wickham and still couldn't understand how Darcy could have treated him so **viciously**.

After a while, Elizabeth began to miss Jane and Charlotte. So, she decided to take a journey of her own. She arrived at Charlotte's new home outside London. Marriage had done very little to change Mr. Collins. Charlotte seemed content, but not exactly happy.

The next night, they took Elizabeth to a party at a nearby estate. Who should she find sitting in the living room, but Mr. Darcy. He was visiting relatives in town and had with him a cousin, Colonel Fitzwilliam.

Darcy greeted Elizabeth awkwardly and didn't say much. When Elizabeth started playing the piano, he walked up and fixed his eyes on her in that same odd stare he had turned on her before. Elizabeth blushed.

"Mr. Darcy, if you are trying to make me nervous, it won't work. I'm always more brave when someone tries to **intimidate** me," she finally said to him.

"I'm sure I'm not trying to frighten anyone, Miss Bennet," he replied. "I have known you long enough now to know that you sometimes misunderstand people."

Elizabeth laughed, though she wasn't sure exactly what he meant. Not knowing what to say next, she turned to Colonel Fitzwilliam.

Heads Up!

Why do you think Darcy says that Elizabeth sometimes misunderstands people? What do you think he is trying to tell her?

"Do you know that the night I met Mr. Darcy, he stood in a corner and didn't talk to anyone."

"But I did not know anyone," Darcy said.

"True," Elizabeth said with a smirk, "and nobody can ever be introduced at a ball."

Darcy smiled. "I don't talk easily with people I don't know."

Elizabeth shrugged and continued to play at the piano. Why, if this man is so unkind, does she seem to enjoy talking to him so? she wondered.

Colonel Fitzwilliam left to get a drink, and Elizabeth spoke to Darcy in a more serious tone.

"You left our town so suddenly last summer," she said. "Does Mr. Bingley plan to return?"

"I doubt it." It was clear Darcy didn't want to talk about it, because he immediately changed the subject. "It looks as if your friend, Charlotte, is happy here," he said.

"I hope so. But I do not think her marrying Mr. Collins was wise," said Elizabeth. "Charlotte married to have a comfortable life even if it does not bring her happiness. But I believe marriage should be for love."

CHAPTER

Darcy's Objections

Who really drove Jane and Bingley apart?

"Miss Bennet, how are you?"

Elizabeth looked up to see Colonel Fitzwilliam walking through the trees. She had gone for a walk in the park near Charlotte's home, eager to read a letter that had just arrived from Jane.

"Are you staying much longer at your friend's?" Fitzwilliam asked.

"I'll be leaving soon," Elizabeth said. "Will you and Darcy be leaving as well?"

"Yes, if Darcy does not put it off again."

"Well, I'm glad you stayed," she said, smiling.

In fact, she had seen Fitzwilliam and Darcy several times and had come to enjoy their company very much. Darcy still didn't speak to Elizabeth much. But he was always polite and his odd stare seemed to follow her around.

Fitzwilliam said, "Next, we are going to see a Mr. Bingley. Do you know him?"

"Oh, yes. He came to our village last spring."

"Perhaps I shouldn't gossip, but I've heard that Darcy has recently saved Bingley from a bad marriage."

Elizabeth suddenly felt her face grow hot with anger. Fitzwilliam was talking about Jane.

"And why did Darcy oppose the marriage?" she asked, trying to keep her voice even.

"Oh, I don't know. There were some objections to the lady."

So it had been Darcy, Elizabeth thought to herself, not Miss Bingley, that drove the two apart. How **pompous** of him to ruin her sister's dreams simply because of his stupid prejudice!

She said abruptly, "I don't think Mr. Darcy should be the judge on matters of love!"

She turned and stalked back to the house.

Heads Up!

What do you think Darcy's objections to Jane were?

CHAPTER

A Poor Performance

Darcy declares his love—sort of.

When Elizabeth got back to Charlotte's, her head was pounding with anger. She went to her room to rest, but it wasn't long before she was woken up by a knock on the door.

She opened it to find Mr. Darcy standing stiffly in the doorway. He walked in, said hello, and sat down. Then he got up again and started pacing the room.

"I have struggled for some time . . . but I cannot change my feelings. Elizabeth, I love you," he said, finally stopping to face her.

Elizabeth could barely believe her ears. Here was a man who thought her sister was not good enough for his friend. How could he be declaring his love for her? It made absolutely no sense to her, and she stared at him coldly.

Elizabeth stares at Darcy coldly. Darcy forces himself to speak.

Darcy went on awkwardly. "I have tried *not* to love you...because of your family. Your family presented...well, obstacles. But even still, I cannot stop thinking of you, Elizabeth, and so I would like you to marry me."

Now Elizabeth got up and began to pace.

"I know I should thank you, but I cannot," she said. "You tell me that my family is not good enough for you! You tell me that you have tried your best *not* to like me. And then you want me to marry you? I will *not!*"

Darcy turned pale and could not speak. He looked angry and embarrassed and forced himself to be calm. "*This* is your reply?" he said. "Will you tell me why you are so unkind?"

"Unkind!" Elizabeth cried. "You are responsible for ruining the happiness of my sister. Do you call that kind?"

Heads Up!

Darcy seems very uncomfortable while he's proposing to Elizabeth. Why? Think of three words to describe him.

"I do not deny that I tried to separate my friend from your sister. And I am happy I succeeded."

Elizabeth glared at him. Finally, she said, "And there is also Mr. Wickham. You caused him such misfortune!"

"I caused *him* misfortune?" repeated Darcy, looking surprised and hurt.

For a moment, Darcy said nothing. Then he took a deep breath and went on, "So according to you, all of this is my fault. But perhaps you are blinded by the fact that I hurt your pride. I am not ashamed of what I said. My concerns about your family are natural and fair. Do you expect me to be happy that you have little money and social position?"

Elizabeth felt herself growing angrier and angrier by the minute.

"No, Mr. Darcy. I don't expect anything of you. No matter how you asked for my hand in marriage, I would not have accepted."

Darcy stiffened and moved toward the door. "You have said enough," he said abruptly. "I understand your feelings. I am now only ashamed of mine. I wish you the best. Good-bye."

Elizabeth watched the door close, then sat down with a tangled mess of thoughts rushing through her head. She could not believe that Mr. Darcy had loved her all this time—that he would want to marry her despite the fact that they came from very different social **classes.** But did that change all the terrible things he'd done—to Mr. Wickham, to Jane? Elizabeth did not know how to feel. She put her head in her hands and began to cry.

Heads Up!

Describe how Elizabeth feels after hearing Darcy's proposal. How would you feel if someone had said those things to you?

CHAPTER

Not Guilty

Darcy explains it all.

Elizabeth woke the next morning feeling confused and went for a walk in the park. She'd only been out a few minutes when Darcy came walking up, looking as though he had barely slept. He gave Elizabeth a letter, mumbled an explanation, then left before she could say a word.

After he had gone, Elizabeth opened the letter and began to read:

Do not worry, Elizabeth. This letter does not repeat our conversation of last night. I only wish to explain some things.

You accused me of two things. One, that I had convinced Mr. Bingley to leave your sister. You must understand that Bingley is a dear friend. I saw how he loved your sister, so I began to watch Jane closely.

She is open and cheerful, but she did not look like she was in love. Perhaps I made a mistake. If she was really in love with him, your anger toward me is understandable. But I only wished to save my friend from an unhappy marriage.

As for Mr. Wickham, it is true that he lived with us. My father paid his expenses, and when my father died, I was to care for Mr. Wickham. But he was lazy and foolish and gambled away a lot of money. When he asked me to pay his debts, I refused, and he left.

Then, last year, he visited my sister, Georgiana, who was only fifteen. He convinced her to run away with him. He did not love her. No, he wanted her fortune, and I saved her just in time.

You may wonder why I did not tell you this last night. I could not find the words then. I wish you the best,

Darcy

Elizabeth read the letter again and again. How differently everything appeared now. It seems that I have been prejudiced too, she thought.

Elizabeth wandered through the fields for many hours. When she got back to the house,

Charlotte told her that Colonel Fitzwilliam and Mr. Darcy had left. Elizabeth, who suddenly felt very lonely, decided to go home as well.

On the way home, her carriage stopped in London to pick up Jane. The sisters talked on the way home. Although Jane had not seen Mr. Bingley while she was in London, Elizabeth was more convinced than ever that her sister was still very much in love with him.

Back at home, everything seemed exactly the same. Lydia was particularly taken by Wickham, which worried Elizabeth. But the soldiers were leaving in a month, so she decided not to tell anyone what she had learned about the man.

Heads Up!

In what ways had Elizabeth been wrong about Darcy? It seems that she had been prejudiced against him. Why?

CHAPTER 11

Fit for a Queen

Elizabeth and Darcy meet face to face again.

Several gloomy weeks passed at home. Elizabeth thought often of Darcy and how she had misunderstood him, but there was no correcting her mistakes now.

The only relief came when her aunt and uncle, the Gardiners, wrote. They asked Elizabeth to join them on a short vacation. Elizabeth jumped at the chance to get away for awhile.

While they were traveling by carriage one day, Mrs. Gardiner said, "You know, Elizabeth, we are not far from Pemberley, the Darcy estate. I believe you know Mr. Darcy, don't you?"

Elizabeth nodded. "Yes. But, we've already seen so many fine houses and interesting places. Surely we don't want to see any more. You must be getting tired."

The thought of running into Darcy, after all that had happened, made Elizabeth feel ill.

"Oh, come Elizabeth, let's go," Mrs. Gardiner said. "Pemberley is one of the grandest places in all of England, and I understand they are happy to show visitors around. It's just too bad that Mr. Darcy won't be there. I have heard he is out of town at the moment. I'm sure you would have liked to see him again."

Elizabeth thought for a moment. If there was no chance of meeting Darcy, perhaps it couldn't hurt to go.

As the carriage entered the Pemberley Estate, Elizabeth gasped. It was an amazing place. A beautiful forest opened up to a wide grassy area. In the distance sat the Pemberley House, a graceful stone building that was so large, it seemed to go on forever.

When they arrived at the house, the housekeeper showed them around. Rooms were decorated in good taste—simple and elegant and fine. For a brief moment, Elizabeth let herself think how wonderful it would be to be the lady of Pemberley Estate.

"Mr. Darcy is expected back tomorrow," the housekeeper said. "Look, there is a portrait of him. Don't you think he's handsome?"

"He is," agreed Elizabeth, looking at the painting. "I knew him a little."

"Then you know he's the kindest of all men. I've never heard a cross word from him in my life. Some people think he acts too proud, but in fact he's too generous and kind."

Elizabeth looked at the portrait. If only she had seen the real Darcy, before it was too late.

As the group was leaving, they took a short walk in the gardens. Elizabeth walked by herself, behind the others, so that she could be alone. As she turned a corner, she suddenly ran into Darcy. Their eyes met, and both of them blushed.

"Oh!" said Elizabeth, in surprise.

Darcy bowed his head and smiled.

Heads Up!

Elizabeth says she knows the real Darcy now. What does she know about him that she didn't know before?

Elizabeth is surprised that Darcy is so polite after everything that has happened.

"You surprised me, Mr. Darcy." Elizabeth could feel her heart pounding. "I heard that you wouldn't be here."

"Yes, I came back a little early. I have guests coming tomorrow, including Mr. Bingley and my sister, Georgiana." He looked nervous and stumbled over his words. "Could I . . . would you . . . may I have the honor of introducing you to my sister?"

"Oh!" Elizabeth said. "Of course." How kind of him, she thought, to be polite after everything that had happened.

"Perhaps you can come back to Pemberley tomorrow?" he asked.

Elizabeth agreed at once. She wanted to say more, to apologize for their misunderstanding. But the Gardiners had turned around, and were waiting for Elizabeth to join them.

Heads Up!

Why is Elizabeth so worried about running into Darcy after their last encounter at Charlotte's? How does she expect Darcy to act toward her?

Darcy walked Elizabeth back to where they were waiting. Then he saw them off in their carriage.

As they drove away, Elizabeth turned and watched out the window as Darcy walked slowly back to his house.

CHAPTER

Snake in the Grass

Wickham strikes again, this time with Lydia.

The next morning, when Elizabeth awoke at her inn, she found a letter from Jane waiting for her. She tore it open and read:

Dear Elizabeth,

Something terrible has happened. Poor Lydia! We have just found out that she has gone off with Wickham. Mother and Father are very upset. If she does not marry, she is ruined forever! Father has gone to London to try to find them. Please pray that all is well.

Yours, Jane

"Oh! Where is my uncle?" cried Elizabeth, darting from her seat. She ran to the door of the inn to go and find him.

At that moment, the door opened and Darcy walked in. She nearly crashed into him.

Elizabeth's pale face made him start, but before he could speak, Elizabeth said, "I'm sorry, I must leave you. I must find my uncle—it's urgent!"

"What is the matter?" he cried. "You look ill."

Darcy listened as Elizabeth poured out the story. "Oh, I have made such a mistake!" she said at last. "I should have warned my sister about Wickham, but I didn't tell anyone."

"No, *I* could have prevented this," Darcy said. "I knew what sort of man he was."

Elizabeth said, "Please forgive me for canceling our plans, Mr. Darcy. I must go home."

Darcy gave her a serious, parting look and went quickly away.

As he left, Elizabeth thought that now, finally, they could never see each other again on such friendly terms. Her family's reputation was ruined, and Darcy would never feel the way he did again. How hard it was to see him go.

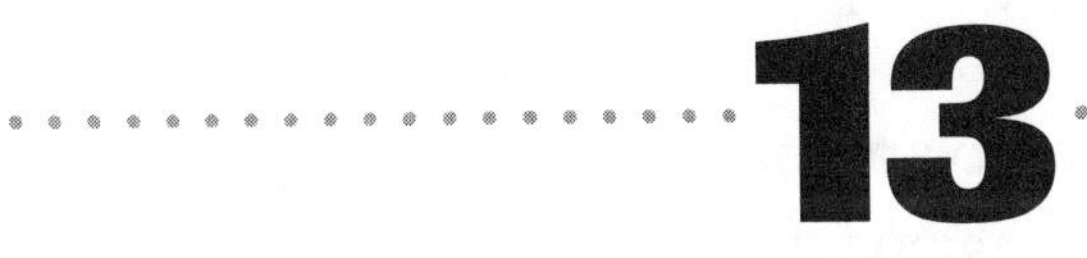

CHAPTER

13

Married Off

The family waits for news and gets plenty!

The Bennet family was gathered round, eager to hear the news. They had been waiting for days, during which time Mrs. Bennet could often be heard weeping uncontrollably in her room.

"Well," said Mr. Bennet, setting a letter from Mr. Gardiner down on the table, "it is settled, for better or worse."

"He has found Wickham and our foolish Lydia," Mr. Bennet went on. "Wickham has agreed to marry her . . . "

Mrs. Bennet squealed with joy, and Mr. Bennet gave her a cold stare before continuing.

"But only if his gambling debts are paid and Lydia receives an allowance. I gather from your uncle's letter that he has taken care of it. Now we must think of how we are going to pay him back."

Mr. Bennet sighed deeply. Mrs. Bennet immediately started planning for the wedding. And Elizabeth once again felt awful to think that she could have prevented it all.

Soon the family received some more news. Mr. Bingley was coming to town once again.

When he arrived to pay a visit to the Bennets, Elizabeth was shocked to see Mr. Darcy with him. The men entered and Jane's face went pale. Elizabeth noticed, though, that Jane's eyes sparkled as she began to talk to Mr. Bingley.

Darcy, however, barely spoke. After all, thought Elizabeth, I cannot expect him to still love me after everything that has happened. The men spent several hours with the Bennets.

After Bingley and Darcy had gone, Jane ran over to Elizabeth.

"Oh, Elizabeth," she said, "how can I bear so much happiness? Mr. Bingley has proposed and I have said yes!"

Elizabeth hugged Jane, who was glowing with joy. Jane looked lovelier than ever.

"He told me that he had loved me from the start," Jane explained, "but that he had been convinced that *I* did not care for him!"

"Yes," said Elizabeth, smiling. "It was a mistake, easily fixed."

"I am the luckiest woman who ever lived!" Jane cried. "If only I could see you as happy!"

When the news reached Mrs. Bennet's ears, she managed to get even more excited than Jane. Imagine, two of her daughters married off in a matter of weeks. Even Mr. Bennet couldn't help but be happy about the latest turn of events. A few weeks before, the Bennets were nearly ruined; now, they were thought to be the luckiest family in the world.

Heads Up!

Elizabeth says the misunderstanding between Jane and Bingley was easily fixed. How do you think it was fixed?

CHAPTER

14

Together at Last

The moment we've all been waiting for.

A most surprising letter came to Elizabeth soon after Bingley's proposal. Mrs. Gardiner wrote to tell Elizabeth a secret: It was Darcy who found Lydia and Wickham, and Darcy who paid the money so that they could be married. He had asked the Gardiners not to tell the Bennets, but now that Mr. Bennet wanted to repay them, Mrs. Gardiner felt it wasn't right to keep Darcy's secret any longer.

Elizabeth was still stunned by Mrs. Gardiner's news when Bingley and Darcy arrived again for another visit. Bingley and Jane walked off together, and Elizabeth suddenly found herself alone with Darcy.

They walked through the fields in silence until finally Elizabeth found the courage to speak.

"For some time, I've wanted to thank you for helping poor Lydia. The rest of my family does not know, but if they did, they would thank you as well."

"Your family owes me no thanks," Darcy said. "I did not do it for them. You must realize that I did it for you."

Elizabeth was too embarrassed to say a word. After a moment, Darcy stopped under an oak tree and looked at her.

"You are too kind to play games with me," he blurted out. "If you still feel the same as you did before, tell me now. My wishes are still the same. But if you do not love me, I'll remain quiet about this forever."

Elizabeth was nearly paralyzed by a rush of feelings. Finally, she opened her mouth and listened to the words come out.

"Most certainly, Mr. Darcy, my feelings have very much changed. I would like nothing more than to be married to you." She looked up to see Darcy break into a broad smile.

They both looked at the ground, embarrassed, for a moment.

"But how can you forgive me after all that I accused you of?" Elizabeth said finally.

"Some of it, I deserved," Darcy replied. "You had bad information, but that wasn't your fault. Did my letter make you think better of me?"

"Yes, it made me understand how very prejudiced I had been."

"As a child," Darcy went on, "I was taught what was right, but I was also taught to be proud. I was taught to care only for my own family and to think ill of the rest of the world. I was this way until I met you, but you have taught me a lesson."

Elizabeth blushed and asked, "Darcy, when did you begin to love me? We did not like each other at first. I was not very nice and neither were you."

"I admired the liveliness of your mind."

"I think you had grown tired of people trying to please you." Elizabeth laughed. "It was my good luck to be so rude."

Heads Up!

What clues were there that they liked each other all along?

Elizabeth blushes and asks Darcy when he began to love her.

Darcy smiled. "Perhaps. But I could see how good you were to your sister. It was obvious that you value the ones you love."

"If you admired me," Elizabeth asked, "then why were you always so quiet? You never looked as if you cared a bit."

"You didn't seem interested."

"But I was embarrassed."

"And so was I."

"If only you'd talked to me more."

"A man who felt less might have talked more."

And speaking like this, they went on walking for hours. They did not pay attention to their direction, or what they passed, or how much time went by. They were too busy to notice such things—they were too busy being in love.

Heads Up!

What traits do Elizabeth and Darcy have in common? What kept them from seeing these things for so long?

Meet the Author

Jane Austen

(1775–1817)

Jane Austen grew up in a family a little like the Bennets. Her father was a minister and provided well enough for his family, but they certainly weren't rich.

When Jane was twenty, she fell in love with a wealthy young Irishman who was visiting England. But his parents decided the Austens weren't good enough for them. Seven years later, Austen got engaged to another rich man, then broke it off because she decided she wasn't in love.

Sound familiar? Both Jane and Elizabeth have the same problems in *Pride and Prejudice.* In their day, love and money were hard to separate, and that's what Austen liked to write about.

Jane Austen was shy about her writing. She never put her name on her books. Today, she's everywhere. Just go to a video store and look up *Pride and Prejudice*, *Emma*, *Persuasion*, and *Mansfield Park.*

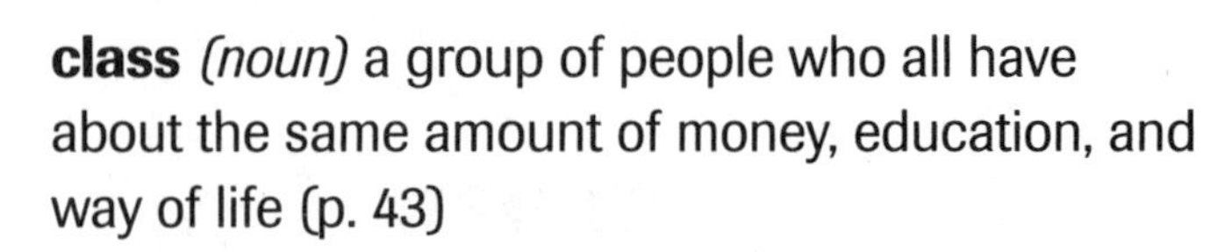
Glossary

class *(noun)* a group of people who all have about the same amount of money, education, and way of life (p. 43)

despise *(verb)* to hate intensely (p. 18)

destitute (*adjective*) poor; not having food or shelter (p. 21)

eligible *(adjective)* being a proper and worthy choice (p. 10)

gentleman *(noun)* a man who is polite, wealthy, and has good manners (p. 17)

inherit *(verb)* to get property or money from someone who has died (p. 19)

intimidate *(verb)* to frighten or bully (p. 35)

manor *(noun)* an estate or a fancy house (p. 8)

prejudice *(noun)* an unfair opinion formed without knowing all the facts (p. 27)

pompous *(adjective)* ridiculously snobby (p. 38)

pride *(noun)* a high opinion of oneself (p. 13)

trudge *(verb)* to walk slowly, with effort (p. 15)

viciously *(adverb)* in a cruel way (p. 34)